This Little Tiger book belongs to:

_____

_____

_____

For Dorcas
L.J.

For Mum and Dad
T.W.

This edition published 2003
First published in Great Britain 1995 by
LITTLE TIGER PRESS
An imprint of Magi Publications
1 The Coda Centre, 189 Munster Road,
London SW6 6AW
www.littletigerpress.com

ISBN 1 85430 915 3
A CIP catalogue record for this book
is available from the British Library
10 9 8 7 6 5 4 3 2 1

tom's tail

Linda Jennings

Tim Warnes

Little Tiger Press
London

Tom's tail was curly like a rolled-up rubber band.
It was a very neat little tail for a piglet.
But Tom thought his tail looked silly.

In all other ways Tom
was a proper little pig.

He was a nice pale pink with dirty patches where he
had wallowed in mud. He slurped and snuffled in the
pig trough with his brothers and sisters and made all
the usual piggy noises.
But how he wished he had a straight tail!

Sam the sheepdog
had a lovely
plumy tail.

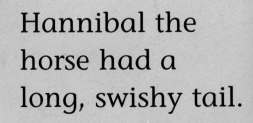

Hannibal the
horse had a
long, swishy tail.

And Geraldine the Jersey cow had a thin, stringy tail with a little tuft on the end.

"Even the rat's tail is nicer than mine," said Tom miserably.

"Why don't you get the tail straightened?" said Hannibal. "How?" asked Tom. "Like this," said Hannibal, and he put his big hoof on the end of Tom's tail. "Now walk away," he said.

Tom squealed and squeaked as he began to walk . . .

. . . his tail stretched out and, when it had uncurled to the very end, Hannibal let go . . .

Ping!

Back sprang the tail . . .

. . . and Tom
hurtled forward . . .

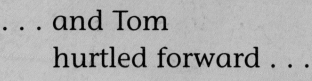

"OUCH!" yelled Tom
and Sam together.

"Tell you what," said Sam, picking himself up.
"Why don't I take hold of your tail and you can
lead me along. That should straighten it!"
So Tom took Sam for a walk, past the pigsties . . .

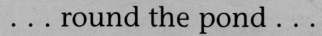

. . . round the pond . . .

. . . and over the buttercup
meadows. "That's enough!"
squealed Tom. "Let me go!"

Ping!

Back sprang the tail to its usual
curly-twirly self. Tom felt miserable.

Geraldine looked at Tom
and chewed thoughtfully.
Suddenly she had a
VERY GOOD IDEA.
She told it to Sam . . .

. . . who took hold of Tom's tail again and stretched it. Then he pushed the tail into a big patch of gooey, squelchy mud! He made Tom lie with his tail covered in mud for an awfully long time, until . . .

. . . the mud dried and Tom's tail
was set into a long, thin pencil.
"YIPPEE!" cried Tom.

He twirled around, trying
to see his new, straight tail.
"OUCH!" said Sam.
Tom had poked him right
in the chest!

"You don't half look silly," said Tom's mother. But Tom liked being different. "I'll wag my tail like Sam does," he said. WHACK!
The tail hit Tom's sister in the face and then prodded his brother in the bottom.
"STOP IT, TOM!" they both cried.

When it was dark, Tom's mother gathered in all her piglets for the night. They liked to snuggle up in a big piggy heap. But Tom's tail got in the way.

"GO AWAY!" cried all his brothers and sisters,
and they chased Tom right out of the sty.

Poor Tom! He tried to curl up outside but it wasn't very comfortable to lie down with a tail as stiff as a pencil. At long last, though, he fell asleep.

In the night it began to rain, but Tom went on sleeping.

As it rained, the hard mud softened and slid off his tail.

By the time morning came, his tail was as curly-twirly as it had ever been.
Grunting happily, Tom went back to the sty.

"Who wants a straight tail, anyway?"
said Tom later, as he pushed into the
trough with all his brothers and sisters.

"Now if I had a long, elegant nose like Hannibal the horse instead of this silly snout, I could *really* get at the food!"

The perfect book for every little piglet!

Smoky Dragons — Jane Clarke, illustrated by Ben Cort

Around the World PiggyWiggy — Christyan and Diane Fox

PIGS CAN'T FLY! — Ben Cort

MOLLY and the STORM — Christine Leeson, Gaby Hansen

Boswell the kitchen cat — Marjorie Newman, illustrated by Suzanne Watts

It's Mine! — Ewa Lipniacka, illustrated by Jane Massey

Hushabye Lily — Claire Freedman, illustrated by John Bendall-Brunello

What Are You Doing in My Bed? — David Bedford, illustrated by Daniel Howarth

For information regarding any of the above titles or for our catalogue, please contact us:
Little Tiger Press, 1 The Coda Centre, 189 Munster Road, London SW6 6AW, UK
Tel: 020 7385 6333 • Fax: 020 7385 7333 • e-mail: info@littletiger.co.uk • www.littletigerpress.com